Augustin Daly

Hazardous Ground

An original adaptation in four acts, from Victoria - Sardon's

Augustin Daly

Hazardous Ground
An original adaptation in four acts, from Victoria - Sardon's

ISBN/EAN: 9783337378585

Printed in Europe, USA, Canada, Australia, Japan

Cover: Foto ©Andreas Hilbeck / pixelio.de

More available books at **www.hansebooks.com**

WEMYSS' ACTING DRAMA.

———◆———

HAZARDOUS GROUND.

An Original Adaptation in Four Acts,

From Victoria Sardon's "Nos Bono Villegeios,"

By AUGUSTIN DALY,

Author of "Under the Gaslight," "Griffith Gaunt," "Taming a Butterfly," etc.

— — — —

AUTHOR'S EDITION.

————

NEW YORK:

W. C. WEMYSS, PUBLISHER,

No. 3 ASTOR PLACE.

1868.

CAST OF CHARACTERS.—[HAZARDOUS GROUND.]

PARK THEATRE, MARCH, 1867.

The Baron..................................... Mr. F. B. CONWAY.

Mons. Macaire [A Parisian —seeking in the village of Bousey, that peace and purity which is said to exist only in the country.]...... Mr. CHIPPENDALE.

Hector Macaire [his Son.]................... Mr. SAVILLE.

The Commissary of Police of the district of Bousey... Mr. STYLES.

Fabbard [Apothecary—chief poisoner of the public mind, and head-centre of the great Bousey Rebellion.]................... Mr. E LAMB.

Granchou [The Village Watchman, and chief of the Fire Department of Bousey.]......... Mr. WREN.

Piparte [The Blacksmith.]...................

Bobosse [Maker of Candies to the youth of Bousey.].................................

Grono [The Gardener.]......................

Perette [The Barber of Bousey.]............. Mr. PARKER.

Pauline [The Baron's Wife.]................ Miss BENEDICT.

Aline [Her Sister.]............................ Miss F. B. CONWAY.

La Mariotte................................... Mrs. HENRI.

Chonchon ....

Mother Perette .... Mrs. HOWARD.

Entered according to Act of Congress, in the year 1863, by W. C. Wemyss, in the Clerk's Office of the United States for the Southern District of New York.

RELATIVE POSITIONS, EXITS, &c.

R., means Right; L., Left; R. H., Right Hand; L. H., Left Hand; C., Centre; S. E., (or 2d E.,) Second Entrance; U. E., Upper Entrance; M. D., Middle Door; F., the Flat; D. F., Door in Flat; R. C., Right of Centre; L. C. Left of Centre.

R.   R. C.   C.   L. C.   L.

*** The reader is supposed to be upon the Stage, facing the audience.

HAZARDOUS GROUND.

ACT 1.

SCENE I.—*Interior of* PERETTE'S *Barber Shop. In* L. F. *an immensely wide window opening upon the Village which is seen beyond. Awning over the window outside. Door in* R. F., *and over fanlight is painted,* PE-RETTE, BARBER. *Cheap prints on the walls—washing place near window. Two low barber chairs,* R. *and* L.

At rise of curtain, one chair is occupied by GRONO, *who is being touched up by* PERETTE, *and the other by a small boy, who is being shampooed by* MOTH-ER PERETTE. PIPARTE *is by window, his feet on ledge, smoking a short pipe, and* BOBOSSE *is seated on a three-legged stool, reading an old paper. Lively music, as a party of gaily dressed villagers pass the window outside—dancing as they go.*

Pip—Say, are you going to keep us all day, and the women off to the festival already?

Per [*To* MOTHER P.] Look sharp, old lady! There's no time to spare; we've got half the villagers to shave yet, and it's nearly ten o'clock.

Moth P If I hadn't commenced to fuss with this little wretch I might have been through with Bobosse and Piparte by this time.

Per You'll never be done till you make that child howl. Stick a little soap in his eye, and you'll find him ready to get up.

Boy You'd better not; my father's head fireman, and he won't see me abused.

Moth P [*Lifting him from chair by hair, and dragging him to basin.*] There, dip your head in that, and keep your mouth shut.

Per Excuse me if I hurry, but on festival day—

Gro Oh, hurry as much as you please; though all I care for is the fireworks, and they don't come off till night.

Moth P [*Back to her chair.*] Now then, whose turn next?

Bob and Pip [*Starting up together.*] Mine!

Moth P [*Stropping razor.*] One at a time! I've got two hands, but only one razor.

Bob [C.] I am the superior in rank; I'm second marshal in the procession.

Pip [C.] I was here first!

Enter Granchou, *in great hurry, divesting himself of his coat and hat.*

Gran Did I hear Mother Perette calling out for a customer?

Pip Yes, and she has two.

Gran All the better for business! [*Seats himself in chair; at each side stand* Bobosse *and* Trpavte.] Come, hurry, or I shan't be in time for the procession.

Pip I beg your pardon! [Granchou *turns and bows politely.*] Bobosse and I were just disputing who should have the chair.

Grin Ah! were you? Well, I'm glad to settle your dispute so easily. I'll take it myself.

Bob But that's not fair.

Gro [*Getting down from his chair.*] Fair or not, I'd like to see you budge Granchou when he's once in possession.

[*Goes up.* Perette *puts away razor, and prepares to go out.*

Pip Oh! I'm not quarrelsome, but the festival—

Gran And what would the festival be without its firemen? and what would the firemen be without me, their chief?

Pip Bah! you and your firemen are all very proud because that aristocrat, the Baron, has given you new hats and an engine! If you were a true villager you'd scorn the gift.

Gran You talk like an idiot! Of course, as independent citizens we scorn the Baron, but as poor firemen we take all we can get.

Bob If it had been Flibbard, he would have treated the gift with lofty contempt.

Gran Ah! but everybody is not a Flibbard.

Pip If we only had him for our mayor, now!

Bob Instead of this haughty Baron—

Pip We would soon take down these aristocrats.

Gran Yes, with Flibbard at our head, and Freedom for our watchword! [*Rising.*] Glorious thought! [Pip *and* Bob *rush for the chair, but* Granchou *re-seats himself.*] No you don't. [*Exit* Groxo, *laughing.*

Moth P Come, come, who is to be shaved?

Pip [*To* Granchou.] Come, give way!

Bob Father Perette, I appeal to you.

Gran This selfishness! Wait till your house burns—

Bob and Pip He threatens us! [*Both fly at him,* Flibbard *enters; nose glass on, pen behind ear, apron in front, no coat, documents in hand.*

Flib Whence this commotion?

Gran, Pip and Bob Mr. Flibbard!

Flib My friends, why will you indulge in these small broils when the great stake is the honor, the virtue, and the prosperity of the whole district of Bousey,—threatened every moment while these aristocrats are in power. We must be firm; we must be active. Our liberties are invaded. Bobosse, you are a confectioner; do the aristocrats of this noble village ever buy their candies of you?

Bob No, they send to Paris for them.

Flib Our domestic products slighted for foreign importations! You, Granchou, are a gardener; does the Baron buy turnips of you?

Gran No; he grows his own cabbages.

Flib Reckless disregard of the commercial interests of the village.

Who have we to thank for all this? Who is the haughty tyrant that grinds us under foot? who is the usurper! An aristocrat! a Baron! Ha! ha! our Mayor! A rich creature who pretends that he is not proud, and insults us by making us gifts, and parades his high birth by being six feet high, when we are only five feet five.

Moth P That's so. Mr. Flibbard!

Flib My friends, I am a man of the people, I am one of you. Heaven has made me more brilliant and talented than you ; education has made me more intellectual ; intermixture with society has made me more polished; but do I scorn you for it ? No! I descend to your level, I mix with you. I say to you, you are my friends, is it not so?

Gran, Pip, and Bob It is! It is!

[FLIBBARD *goes up and sits in* MOTHER P's *chair, as others gaze at him.*

Flib Come, let us be shaved ; the hour passes.

Moth P Directly, sir.

Flib Not you, old woman! Where is your husband? I am a man, and must be shaved by my equal.

Gran, Pip, Bob Noble sentiment! [*Exchange looks of admiration.*

Per [*Going off* R. C.] Excuse me, Mr. Flibbard, but I have to go out, to shave Mr. Morrison, at the new cottage.

Flib Morrison, the Parisian, the neighbor of the Baron ?

Gran The new aristocrat, who is so rich and so proud?

Per That's the one, neighbor.

Flib Stay, misguided man! Shave the friend of the people, and let the aristocrats import their barbers, as well as their candies.

Gran, Pip, and Bob Beautiful sentiment! [*Same play as before.*

Per Yes, it's a beautiful sentiment, but the money I shall get will be better.

Flib [*Sentimentally.*] Lost to patriotism! Lost!

CHONCHON, *very frowsy and girlish, entering ; plenty of ribbons.*

Cho [*Running against* PERETTE.] O, you are always in the way.

Per Well, what do you want ?

Cho I want my waterfall I left yesterday to be frizzed. [*Turns and sees* GRANCHOU *and* BOBOSSE *grinning, and bowing to her.*] La! are you there?

Per I don't know anything about your waterfall. Mother Perette, attend to this goose. [*Exit* R. C.

Gran How lovely you look this morning.

Bob You will be the belle.

Gran You will dance with me.

Cho I shall be very glad, I'm sure, if I get my waterfall.

Moth P Come, I'll get it for you. Don't stand fooling there, you little imp. Lord! just out of short clothes, and making eyes at the men already.

[*Exit* CHONCHON *in sweet confusion, after* MOTHER P., L. 2 E. *The men having bowed her out, come down nudging each other.*

Flib Friends, do not permit the blandishments of women to blind you to your nobler duties. [*They become grave instantly.*] Women are beautiful, but they have no vote. Therefore, useless, and to be disdained.

All Beautiful sentiment! [*Same play*].

Flib One more danger threatens. The aristocrats have even engrossed our friend, the barber. Ah! if he were a true patriot what a service he could render. Summoned to the Baron—for instance—as a barber, he would have the usurper in his power. The idea is appalling, but vast. [GRANCHOU *feels his throat uneasily.*

Gran Yes, too vast; don't let us think of it.

Pip And then who would succeed him!

All Ah! who?

Flib Is there no one you can think of?

Bob [*Timidly.*] Granchou!

Flib [*Hastily.*] An excellent man! but too fiery! too hasty. We want caution. [*Shakes* GRANCHOU *affectionately by the hand.*

Gran Piparte, hey!

Flib [*Same.*] A great man! a great man! But the cares of politics —too exciting! It would kill him. [*Same play with* PIPARTE.

Pip How about yourself, Mr.——?

Flib My friends, language fails me in acknowledging the great honor you have done me. To be named by you as the successor of the Baron, as your future mayor, is dignity enough. But to be thus nominated, without a dissenting voice, is a glorious answer to my detractors and calumniators, wherever and whoever they may be. I accept the important trust you have confided to me. You shall be a happy and united people. I—excuse these tears! My friends—my friends—

[*Drops his arm on* GRANCHOU'S *shoulder, and buries his head in it as he grasps* PIPARTE *by the hand.*

Bob But the Baron is mayor yet.

Flib That word recalls me. I am a man again. Let the Baron look to himself.

Gran Ah! I can take care of him. If I should only spread a certain report concerning him and his household, he would soon be glad to fly from *our* scorn and leave the field to us.

All A report!

Gran Yes, of what happened in his garden last night.

Flib His garden!

Pip and Bob Last night!

Gran [*After assuring himself that they are alone.*] I was crossing his grounds about eleven o'clock last night, to go and fish in his pond, when there jumped over the wall of the private garden, and upon me—a young man!

Flib A villager!

Gran A Parisian—I know by his boots—I felt them.

Flib And his face——

Gran I couldn't see it. As I was picking myself from the ground he knocked my hat over my eyes and was gone.

Flib Humph!

Gran An hour later I again came upon him. I caught at his coat, and he knocked me into the water. When I crawled out, the Baron's wife was just disappearing among the trees, near the house, and the young man was gone. [*All look at each other.*

Flib [*Using snuff-box.*] The Baron's wife! Are you sure? It might have been her sister. You know they are both young, and about the same height.

Gran Well, I only saw her walk, and it might have been——

Flib [*Looking around at them.*] No; the sister has no lover! If she had, he would come to see her in broad day. The young man who jumps over a wall at midnight comes after another sort of person. I always find that men risk their necks for what they ought not to have.

Gran It must have been the wife.

Flib This is a serious business. Our purity is invaded. Friends— as members of the common council of Bousey, I address you. [*They straighten up.*] Is this degradation to be permitted? Who is this culprit—this young man? Have you no clue, Granchou?

Gran I found in the grass by the pond a hat dropped by the Parisian in his fright. [*Produces it from his breast.*

Flib An important detail ; Guard it carefully, and let us look carefully in the festival to-day, for the owner.

Enter LA MARIOTTE, R. C., *smartly dressed, bustling, and goes down to chair, seizes razor. and begins stropping. Dialogue through business. All the men cluster round her.* CHONCHON, *who appears at* L. 2 E., *with enormous waterfall on, is quite neglected.*

La M Good morning, friends. All waiting for me. Well, I'll be ready in a turn.

Cho Ahem! ahem! [*Fixing waterfall, no attention paid to her.*

Flib [*To* LA M.] My child, you look charming.

Gran I am down for the first three dances with you at the ball to-night, you know.

Flib You are to sup with me, you know.

Bob You'll be the prettiest girl out to-day.

Cho Oh! the wretches. I say, Mariotte, you are very busy there, aint you? he! he!

La M Yes, wouldn't you like to help me a little at this sort of work, Chonchon?

Cho Ugh! you ugly thing! Everybody is pulling at your skirts— you won't keep them clean long, I'm afraid.

Gran [*Going up*] Why, Chonchon.

Cho [*Boxing his ears.*] Get out of the way.
[*Exit, with her waterfall coming off.*

La M Now then, whose turn first? [*Rolls up her sleeves and takes up the lather.*] I'm ready to go to work—who is it?

All I! I! [*Grand rush.*

Flib [c.] One moment! Rank takes precedence everywhere. The future mayor is to be shaved first.

Gran But I thought you insisted on being shaved by an equal!

Flib Well, Mariotte may not be an equal, but she's a good match for any man.

La M [*Making lather vigorously.*] Bring on the mayor, then. I'm ready for him.

[*FLIBBARD takes chair with grace. In all the following scene, FLIBBARD endeavors to preserve easy grace, while LA M. is brusque and mischievous.*

Gran Do hurry up, Miss Mariotte.

Pip It is already time we were off

Bob The festival will begin without us.

Flib [*Who is now entirely lathered, scoops out place to talk, and bolts up.*] The festival cannot begin without its grand marshal.

[*LA M. pulls him back, and strops razor to begin.*

Gran But the young man may escape us.

Flib [*Same play.*] If he escapes to-day, we will find him to-night.

La M Do be quiet.

[*Same play—takes him by the nose and commences to shave.*

Gran Yes, in the Baron's garden—he is sure to be there again.

La M [*Pausing, and holding nose.*] What are you talking about? The Baron's garden—to-night—a young man?

Gran Perhaps it's your beau; you wait on the Baroness every night. Does your beau jump over the Baron's garden wall?

La M No, nor no other person.

Gran Oh! but I beg your pardon; I saw him.

Flib Excuse me, if this parley is to continue, will you release my nose.

La M When did you see a young man?

Gran Last night. I saw him, and I felt him.

La M It is false, I say it is false. You vile slanderers—

Flib Be calm, my child! It is not you who are compromised.

La M Who, then?

Flib Who but that importer of foreign vices, the corrupter of social morals—the Baroness.

La M [*Menacing him with razor.*] The Baroness! I'd as lief you'd abuse me as her. I ought to cut your nose off this moment, you old wretch! FLIBBARD *starts up in alarm; the others also scatter in dismay, as she menaces them.*] And all of you! you prying, cowardly, slanderous brutes. The baroness is as virtuous as she is generous; and the Baron is too noble and good to be abused. What have they both not done for you and your children and the poor of the place?

[*Threatening, c.*

Flib [L. C.; *Others huddled about him.*] Councilmen of Bousey be firm! Why, Mariotte, there would be nothing strange if the Baroness did have a beau. The Baron is twice his wife's age.

La M Yes, he's forty and she's twenty, and they love each other so that I begin to think that is the right sort of match after all. [*Throwing away razor, and turning down sleeves.*] There. You may go without shaving to-day, or scrape yourselves. I won't ever touch one of you again. And I'll go and warn the Baroness of your spying and lies into the bargain. [*Exit.*

Flib [*Still lathered, c.*] We are safe. This girl is in league with the enemy; but we must form a plan. We must devote ourselves to th task. Let us watch the Baron's park night and day, especially . night. This young man will go there again. I have always found that when a young man ought not to go somewhere again, he does. You Granchou, and you, my friends, must watch the house; I will aid you. To-night we will begin. If we discover the villain we raise the neighborhood and cover the aristocrat with the shame that must ensue. Then, the municipal reform is complete. We regenerate Bousey. Is it agreed?

All It is.

Flib Swear.

All We swear.

[*Very distant festival music.* HECTOR *appears at back, looking about him. Seen through window.*

Flib [*Looking back.*] Sh! a stranger! A fop! no doubt a Parisian, one of our hereditary foes.

Gran [*Same.*] Ha! [FLIB *and others look at him.*] That coat—I know that coat. The garden wall last night!

Flib The cap! [GRANCHOU *produces it.*] We will try it on him!

Enter HECTOR, *sauntering; the others retreat,* L.

Hec This is the shop, but where is the pretty maid? [*Sees others, and bursts out laughing at* FLIBBARD, *who tries to wipe his face.*] Who the deuce have we here? He looks like one of the Alpine hills, whose summit is covered with snow.

[FLIBBARD *assumes an air of dignity and suavity, and he and* GRANCHOU *approach* HECTOR, GRANCHOU *holding the cap behind him.*

Flib Good morning, sir. You are just arrived in our village?

Hec [*Looking suspiciously at him.*] Yes.

Flib This morning, perhaps.

Hec Perhaps.

Flib Then you have not been able to see all the beauties of the place. The women of Bousey are said to be lovely.

Hec I'm glad to hear it, for the sake of the men of Bousey.

GRAN. *crosses to other side and behind him.*

Flib And our streets! our cottages! our *parks*—and *gardens!*

Gran Particularly the Baron's!

[HECTOR *looks from one to the other, then shrugs his shoulders.*

Flib By night, the parks are superb.

Gran Yes; about eleven at night!

[HECTOR *glances fiercely at each.*

Flib But in visiting the parks it is necessary to have a large collection of hats—one is so apt to lose them when jumping the walls.

[*Music increasing.*

Hec Fellow! [*Aside.*] Am I known, then? Have they recognized me?

Flib Your hat does not seem to fit you; we have excellent hatters in Bousey. Granchou, can't you supply the gentleman?

[HECTOR *turns fiercely on* GRAN., *who presents hat.*

Gran Try this one. [HECTOR *starts.*] I found it last night, in the garden walk, near the fish-pond, about eleven!

Hec [*Seizing the hat, and choking* GRANCHOU.] Rascal! don't breathe another word, or I'll choke you. [*Relaxing—and low.*] Say nothing of this, and if you want money— [*Puts hand in pocket.*
Flib [*Restraining him*] We are members of the Common Council, and are not to be bought! [HECTOR, *in rage, takes* R. *corner.*
Gran [*Crossing to others,* L.] It is he.
Hec [R. c.] Hark ye! my good fellows! you all seem to be engaged in this little comedy. Now, listen to me. If any of you—or you, or you, [*Pointing his finger at each.*] even cross my road, or breathe a word of me to a single soul, I'll make dead men of you, and put a monument over your graves, inscribed to the memory of meddlers.
[*Music, forte.*
Flib The safety of Bousey calls us, my friends! let us go!
[*The village girls seen at the opening, repass at back with wreaths and banners. The conspirators rushing for entrance,* R. C., *encounter* HECTOR, *who stands in doorway, barring their exit, and bowing to girls. Misery of the conspirators.*   *Scene closed in.*

SCENE II.—*The* BARON'S *grounds, with view of Mansion in distance through trees. The wall of the private garden at* R. *and* L. *Overhanging trees, and little green gate; cut wood,* 1st *grove—twilight.*

Enter BARON, *very richly dressed, with cane; followed by old* MACAIRE, *with fishing rods, flies, and other fancy traps and basket,* L. 1 E.

Bar So you've had poor luck with your line?
Mac Several bites, but not a catch. I was worried to death by the villagers, who seemed to think my fishing in the waters an outrage.
Bar Yes, they consider that such easements should be enjoyed by us with anything but ease. I tell you, neighbor, one must come to the country to know it. Until I lived in this village I never rightly appreciated the people of the rural districts. Now I do. Such is their love of virtue that they condemn everything from the city indiscriminately, until they succeed in imitating it. My poor wife came here a month ago from her tour of the Pyrenees with her sister. Bousey howled at the length of their trains, and the style of their hair; and the week after every woman of the place had a train twice as long, and enough curled hair on to stuff a sofa.
Mac [*Laughing.*] Only tell Hector all this, and he will devise some plan to pay back your mischievous friends, I'll warrant.
Bar Oh! Hector is your son, of whom you have spoken to me. Has he arrived yet?
Mac This morning only, fresh from Paris, and came directly to me. Ah! he loves me so much.
Bar He is a student still?
Mac No, already a lawyer, and only twenty-four.
Bar You must bring him to the house. I shall be glad to know him.
Mac A splendid fellow. So noble! so ingenuous—so truthful —so light-hearted, and not a vice; think of that—not a vice,

and twenty-four. But, [*Confidentially.*] He, he—he is in love! Yes, in love. He confessed all to me. A charming creature, brunette, young, lovely—but then he sighed as he described her.

Bar [*Smiling.*] Ah! she does not return his passion.

Mac Oh, yes—but an obstacle. I tried to get him to say what kind of an obstacle, but he wouldn't. Then, there is a complication, too.

Bar A complication!

Mac Yes; it seems that the young lady has a sister, and this sister loves him, and it seems he has been so agreeable to the sister—

Bar That she fancies he loves her alone!

Mac Exactly; two sisters and only one beau. It is terrible.

Bar No, it is laughable. Which does he love best?

Mac I don't believe he could tell himself.

Bar Well, well, we shall soon know. We will subject him to the scrutiny of the Baroness, who is very sage, and to Aline, who is very roguish, and then we must see whether this obstacle can't be removed.

Mac That is the Baroness herself who comes yonder, is it not?
[*Looking* R. 1 F.

Bar [*Same.*] No, but simply, the best little woman in the world—

Enter PAULINE. R. 1 E., *with light scarf over shoulders, and in elegant walking dress.* MACAIRE *removes his hat and bows.* BARON *holds out both hands-smilingly, and she goes to him.*

Bar How lovely you do look, to be sure.

Pau That is the tenth time you have told me so to-day. Good day, Mr. Macaire; have you been fishing on this great festival day in Bousey?

Mac I have been trying to fish, madame.

Pau [*To* BARON.] And you—why are you not on the great square, receiving the plaudits of the firemen at the head of their new engine?

Bar My dear child, I have just returned from my triumphal reception. They cheered me until they were hoarse, but from the loudness of the shouts, I felt that the cries came from their lungs, and not from their hearts. Is luncheon ready?

Pau [*Who has been looking round absently.*] Yes, Aline will be there to pour out your chocolate.

Bar Who are you looking for?

Pau Oh! I!—no one—for Aline. She promised to overtake me here.

Bar Then how is she to pour out my chocolate, if she is to meet you here?

Pau She and I will return together.

Bar Then you will both pour out my chocolate, and I shall be the best served gentleman in France. Come, neighbor, let us discuss Bousey together over a cup of chocolate.
[*Exeunt through gate,* PAULINE *looking after them*

Enter HECTOR, L, 2 E.

Hec [*Cautiously.*] Are you alone?

Pau Imprudent one! You here again, and so near the house?

Hec Oh, there is nothing to fear, it is only at night there is danger.

Pau You were not seen last night?

Hec Quitting the park after the interview I stole so cunningly from you—the first since your flight from me, two months ago, I saw the watchman—

Pau [*Excited.*] He discovered you?

Hec No, but as I leaped the wall near the stream I tumbled on a man fishing.

Pau And then?

Hec And then—I tossed him into the water, and escaped without being recognized.

Pau Thank Heaven! and now, sir, you must come here no more. Nay, you must keep in your house all day, lest you should be identified by those who saw you.

Hec Have no fear. We are safe. But I must see you again.

Pau No! no!

Hec Yes, to-night. I will steal over the little gate again and meet you.

Pau You dare not, sir!

Hec Ah, what is there love does not dare.

Pau Never mention love to me again. I fled from you before when you were pursuing me with your attentions ; yesterday you appeared before me, having tracked me home. I have never been culpable until last night, when I consented to speak with you alone, thinking to persuade you to leave me at peace. I will not be culpable again, neither to-night, nor to-morrow, nor ever. We shall see each other no more.

Hec At least—

Pau Farewell.

Hec No, not farewell—for we *shalll* meet again.

Pau Do not think it.   [*Exit through gate.*

Hec [*Solus.*] Of course she couldn't say less than that. She must be coy and backward. But then she remains so—just as when I met her in the Pyrenees—spent a month in her society, and thought myself in heaven every time she smiled towards me, but never anything but a smile ; no impression in the world *apparently.* But she fled from me. That told me she feared to trust herself, and said to me all that is needed is perseverance. Then I find her here—coy and backward, and still the same disposition to fly, and no disposition to tell her husband or her sister. Her sister ! Aline ! rosy, happy, roguish ! Now, how the deuce was it that I didn't fall in love with Aline ? At least I did all I could. I pretended to in order to be in Pauline's company on our travels. Innocent little saint ! It would be most despicable in me to deceive her any more. At least I can keep out of her way.

Aline [*Outside*, L. 2 E.] Baron! Baron! wait a minute, I'm out of breath.

Hec Fate! Too late! [ALINE *runs in, her hat hanging by ribbon from her neck, ribbons streaming, dressed in white.*

Ali Oh! Baron, I thought you were lost.

Hec For a Baron lost, behold a lover found!

Ali [*Joyfully.*] Oh, is it you? Is it really you?

Hec It is I.

Ali What a surprise! Oh, I'm so glad to see you again.

Hec Of course you say so because I have come.

Ali [*Primly.*] Really! [*As before.*] You have not forgotten me, then?

Hec To be sure I've not.

Ali I waited so long for you.

Hec [*Surprised.*] Waited?

Ali For eight days after we went away from you so suddenly in the mountains, you never left my mind.

Hec It was a magnetic feeling.

Ali But come into the house; we ought not to stop here to talk like two neighbors, at a gate.

Hec But I like to,—and we are neighbors. My father lives just over there. [*Pointing* L.

Ali Mr. Macaire?

Hec Yes.

Ali [*Clapping her hands.*] O-o-h! Do you know I was twenty times on the point of asking him if he was not your father, but I was so afraid? I tried, but I became red all at once; but we are great friends.

Hec I made him buy his little house.

Ali So as to be here?

Hec Of course.

Ali Oh, that is so nice! From my chamber I can look into your garden.

Hec You are on the first floor.

Ali No, that is my sister's room, all at the left.

Hec Pauline's?

Ali Yes, just over the garden.

Hec [*Aside.*] Ah! very well.

Ali And now tell me—sh! ever so low,—tell me, have you not said anything to your father of me,—nothing—nothing?

Hec [*Smiling*] Not yet. To-morrow.

Ali You think I won't please him?

Hec Ah! what an idea. You!

Ali It must have been instinct, for do you know that every time I met him I answered his salutation with my prettiest smile—and I can smile prettily when I want to, can't I? [HECTOR *kisses her hand.*] When he came to pay my sister his visit of welcome, I tried so to please him, I was so amiable, and so nice,—Oh! you don't know how gracious I was. [*Nestling nearer* HECTOR.] for it seemed to me that a voice said to me, "Aline, try and please this man, for he will make your happiness," and I believe I succeeded.

Hec I'm sure you did.

Ali Besides, he is so good.   I'm sure he indulges you.

Hec A little.

Ali And you abuse it.   [*Parts from him.*

Hec Sometimes.

Ali Fie! that's wrong.   See there how hard it is for one to show how much they love.   See what comes of it.   I know, so I dissimulate with you.   I make believe I don't care.

Hec Yes, you keep me at a distance ; you are always cold.

Ali [*Running to him.*] Me! why I thought I was too bold.

Hec Ah! that—

Pauline [*Outside.*] Aline!

Ali It is sister calling.   I am going.

Hec Already!   [ALINE *runs out through gate.*] What a darling little saint!   Can I resist loving her? but then—

> [ALINE *appears looking over the wall.*

Ali Go round by the walk, there; sister will introduce you to the Baron.

Hec [*Quickly.*] No, no! not yet.

Ali [*Pouting.*] Why not?

Hec I will tell you some other time—to-morrow.

Ali But I must tell my sister I have seen you.

Hec Why, what need of that?

Ali Oh! I don't like to fib ; and then what good are these mysteries?   We have built up a crowd of projects.   You are a young gentleman, I am a young lady ; you are going to ask for my hand ; it will be given to you, and we will be happy.   Is not all that natural and simple?

Hec Yes, yes.

Ali Well, then I will go and tell my sister all.   [*About to go.*

Hec [*Quickly.*] Not to-day, I beg of you.

Ali [*Stopping.*] But when?   When will you come and be presented?

Hec As soon as I can.

Ali To-morrow, then.

Hec To-morrow, yes, to-morrow.

Ali With your father.   Well, take the key.   [*Throws it to him.*

Hec The key?

Ali Yes, of this little green gate.   It shortens the walk for you, [*Archly.*] and as I hope that after this you will come every day, and oftener—

Hec Oh, indeed I will.

Ali [*Pouting.*] Because I don't like to see you this way by stealth. We have the air of loving on the verge of an abyss.

Hec Just as we used to on the Pyrenees.

Ali At the Pyrenees you gave me your arm, and here you do not even give me your hand.

Hec Oh yes, but I will—   [*Running to her.*

Ali Don't! I don't want you to.

Hec Oh yes!

Ali No, I'm going to run away.   Don't look that way.   You look

a, if you'd eat me. [*Whispers, as* HECTOR *turns away.*] Hector, I'm going, I'm going. [*Disappears, laughing.*
Hec By Jove, when I'm with her a quarter of an hour, it is she alone that I love. [*Pause.*] A reasonable man would not hesitate. He would close his heart to the guilty love, and open it to the pure which offers itself to him so gently. But I'm not a reasonable man. Where is the key? [*Picks it up.*] Who ever heard of a young fellow of twenty-three who was reasonable? And yet Aline! But I have the key, and to-night,—I leave the rest to to-night. [*Exit* L. 2 E.

ACT II.

S C E N E.—*Drawing Room at the* BARON'S *house.* *Open doors* C. *and* R. *and* L. C., *leading to grounds and terrace.* *Doors to inner apartment,* R. *and* L. *Table* O. *It is dark, and there are three lamps lighted about the place. On* L. *table, with* BARON'S *hat and cane. Lounge* R. *At table supping choco-late,* PAULINE, *the* BARON *and the* COMMISSARY.

Bar And so you have to go to the next village, Mr. Commissary of Police.
Com Yes, a dark affair. A jealous husband, who killed a lover of his wife with a scythe.
Pau How horrible! and the wife——
Com Oh! he did nothing to her.
Bar That was wrong; because the most criminal of the two was the woman.
Com Then *you* would have spared the lover?
Bar Oh, no! the woman first—the lover next; or, even both at once. Your man was a blunderer; while he was in for it he should have done for both at once.
Com You are ferocious! Does the Baroness recognize her hus-band under this aspect?
Bar She is of my opinion. Is it not so?
Pau Doubtless!
Bar Why, what is the matter, my dear? you are pale?
Pau Yes, this headache which will not leave me, and the odor of the cigar——
Bar [*Rising.*] Ah, I ask pardon, my darling. I forgot we were in your room, and two paces from your chamber.
Pau No, stay where you are, I will go out in the air.
[*Exit through grounds.*
Com What a splendid necklace the Baroness has on.
Bar Yes, that amiable Flibbard enlarges upon them in his speeches to the Common Council, on "Luxury in High Places."

ALINE *entering,* L.

Ali Where is Pauline?

Com Good evening, Madamoiselle.

Bar Your sister is in the park, to take the air. Do you know, my darling, that she does not go to the ball?

Ali [*Pouting.*] Then I will go with old Madame Boutille.

Bar That will do, and I will go to bed.

Ali And let all the villagers say you were too proud to come to their ball. You think you are too popular already ; do you?

Bar You are right. Well, I will go.

Ali And you must dance.

Bar O, by Jove!

Ali Yes, you must ; just as I'm going to [*With an air.*] out of devotion to the municipal cause.

Com It would be a popular movement, Baron.

Bar Well, then, I will dance.

Ali Ah ! I knew you would. And I'll run off and finish my toilet. But you needn't wait for me. Good bye. [*Kissing him.*] How funny it will be to see you dance with Chonchon.

[*Exit, laughing.*

Com And I am off to my unpleasant duty.

Bar Come back to the ball when you get through and we will sup together.   [*Exit* COMMISSARY POLICE, R. C.

Enter LA MARIOTTE, L.

La M Oh, Mr. Baron, there is a deputation outside come to wait on you.

Bar A deputation !

La M Yes, of the Common Council.

Bar Good. Let them in, and lock up the spoons.

Enter FLIBBARD, GRANCHOU, *drunk, between* BOBOSSE *and* PIPARTE.

Bar Well, gentlemen.

Flib Mr. Mayor, we have come——

Gran Hear ! hear !

Pip Hush !

Gran Silence ! Question ! Down with aristocrats ! Who has got the floor ? Motion.

Bar I think, my good fellow, as you seem to have the floor, you had better make a motion—towards the door.

Flib [*To others, aside.*] Take that fool out.

Gran No, sir ! I will not, sir !

Bar [*Going to table and taking his cane.*] You will not?

Gran Yes, sir, I will, sir! A sense of duty to myself calls me away.

[*Exit with* PIPARTE *and* BOBOSSE.

Bar Ah, you remain, Mr. Apothecary !

[LA MARIOTTE *closes door at back, and exits.*

Flib I remain, Baron, for I have some serious things to say.

Bar [*Going to table and lighting cigar.*] Ah ! Do you smoke ?

Flib A thousand thanks, Baron. I never tried but once—ah ! the very thought——

Bar [*Sitting.*] Well, sir, and your errand.

Flib To come to the point, I am delegated, Baron, by the notables of the village, to express to you with every delicacy, the profound antipathy you inspire throughout the district.

Bar Thank you for your delicacy. So I inspire antipathy, do I?

Flib O, tremendous! But it is not to be avoided. There are some faces that we will not take to—while others—for instance mine! I have only to make my appearance; they adore me!

Bar It is a gift of nature, Flibbard.

Flib A gift of nature.

Bar Well, to come to the end. You came to propose——

Flib I came to propose to you in good faith, Mr. Mayor, that you should hand in your resignation.

Bar Well, and if I yield to this desire—my successor; may I ask —who—will it be you?

Flib It will be I. I lead the people. They adore me. You were not at my last conference.

Bar No.

Flib So much the worse for you. It was a scene. I had some moments of inspiration. [*Taking up position.*] Thus, when I turned with a menacing gesture towards the bad and mighty city, like this.

Bar No! to the left. The mighty city is upon your left.

Flib No; to the right.

Bar Pardon me; to the left.

Flib Never mind; I menaced this side, anyway.

Bar Oh, then you only menaced the insignificant huts at the bottom of my garden.

Flib [*Sittling.*] It matters little.

Bar On the contrary, Mr. Flibbard, since my arrival here I have seen that Bousey was too narrow for our two ambitions. We are here, we two, like Cæsar and Pompey in Rome.

Flib [*Slapping his breast in pronouncing the name of Cæsar.*] Like Cæsar and Pompey, that's the word.

Bar And as we have no armies, we will fight alone. Which do you prefer, tomahawks or bludgeons?

Flib [*Starting up.*] Sir, we are not red Indians.

Bar You will not consent.

Flib As a man, perhaps I might, but as an apothecary—the spirit of my order will not permit me.

Bar But I refuse to resign to you.

Flib You must. Do not wrestle with fate. The Council are all with me. Being a doctor, I hold the members by their infirmities. Granchou by his lumbago, Bobosse by his mumps, Piparte by the teething of his youngest child, Perette by his cramps. Vote for me, I say, or I resign you to your agonies! Look at this.

[*Producing paper.*

Bar A prescription for the mumps?

Flib A petition of the whole Municipal Council for your removal. Resign, and you will spare its transmission.

Bar Let me see it.

Flib [*Reading.*] "Monsieur Le Prefect."

Bar Ah! it is to the Prefect of Police.

Flib To the Prefect! [*Continuing reading.*] "In presence of the scandalous events which afflict the district of Bousey, we hope that the Mayor—"

Bar Stop! what scandalous events?

Flib [*Smiling.*] Ah, that belongs to another order of delicate things.

Bar What things? Tell me!

Flib I—I—really, it is unfortunate, the poverty of our language is such that it can't express a thing which is all over town.

Bar [*Losing patience.*] You are mocking me, Mr. Flibbard.

Flib [*Frightened*] No, no! I am not. He will strangle me.

Bar Will you tell me, then, once for all?

Flib Never! I will rather leave to events the duty of instructing you. Let us return the petition. Shall I send it?

Bar [*Taking it.*] Let me see it.

Flib [*Sentimentally.*] You will spare us then the sorrow—

Bar We shall see. In any case, the Prefect ought to see this precious document. Only, let us complete it, for I don't see your signature.

Flib You understand my delicacy, Baron.

Bar [*Going to table.*] We must do things regularly. Here is a pen. Sit.

Flib [*Sits.*] As you like.

Bar [*Picking up cane as if unconsciously.*] And write here, I pray you, "All the signers of this petition—"

Flib The signers? they are the Common Council—

Bar I know; go on; "All the signers of this petition, members of the Common Council of Bousey—" [FLIBBARD *repeats writing.*] "are rascally knaves."

Flib [*Jumping.*] What!!

Bar "Rascally knaves."

Flib This outrage, sir, to my party—

Bar [*Tranquilly,—playing with cane.*] Remember, it is I that am Cæsar.

Flib [*Intimidated.*] It is written! It is written! [*Aside, as he writes.*] I won't send it, that's all.

Bar Sign it.

Flib Is that necessary, too?

Bar [*Cane play.*] Oh, let us sign, I beg. [FLIBBARD *signs.*] That's it. [*Takes paper.*

Flib How?

Bar [*Looking over it.*] "All rascally knaves,—Flibbard." This testimony of the character of the Council, from you, my dear Mr. Flibbard, is worth gold.

Flib [*Frightened.*] You are not going to send it?

Bar Never doubt me. [*Rings—enter.* LA MARIOTTE.] *Show Mr. Flibbard out.* Ha! ha! Give my compliments to the Common Council, and don't forget—I am Cæsar. [*Exit to* L.

La M Now, sir, as soon as you are ready.

Flib [*About in consternation*] I'm in a blaze.

Bob [*Appearing at back* R.] Psitt!   [LA MARIOTTE *jumps.*

Pip [*At* L. *back.*] Psitt!   [LA MARIOTTE *jumps.*

Gran [*At* c.] Psitt! [*Comes down with precaution, others following.*]
Well, has he bitten?

Flib Bitten! Yes, to the bone. But only wait, I'll make such a row for you with your wife, my fine Baron, that you will be glad to pack off. Come, to our posts, to watch. Everybody is going to the festival dance but the Baroness. Our lover will not miss the opportunity to introduce himself here, as he did last night.

[*Exeunt all,* c. *&* n.

La M [*Following and closing the doors.*] Some of our Common Council is very drunk; but I suppose that's nothing singular.

Ali [*Outside, calling.*] Pauline! [*Entering.*] Pauline! where can she be? [*Trumpet heard.*

La M Lord! there's the trumpet, and they are commencing to dance without me.

Ali What a misfortune! Has everybody gone?

La M Long ago, Miss, and all kicking up their heels by this time at the ball.

Ali Well, if all is fastened, you may go too.

La M Thank you. Good dancing, Miss. [*Exit* L.

Ali Dear! I'm all alone. If I was coward,—but I'm not a coward. I wish Madame Boutelle would come. If the air was not so fresh I'd go to seek Pauline, while waiting for her. B-r-r-r! Where did I put my book? I will read a little. [*Looking for it.*] When I say I will read, I mean if I can, for since the last three months, when I try to read, my eyes go the one road, and my thoughts all go another. I turn over the leaves, but at the head of every chapter there is always the same word, Hector! All the characters, Hector! all the words, Hector, Hector, Hector! and it's wrong. I have scolded myself for it. Where *have* I put my book? At least, I will turn over the pages. Ah! in Pauline's chamber, on the round table. [*Exit* R. 1 E.

Enter HECTOR, C., *cautiously.*

Hec No one here. Not a soul to be seen. The Baron is at the ball, and doubtless she is alone [*Looking* R.] in her chamber. This is an audacious act of mine, and will bear as little light as possible. [*Puts out two lamps, and while at the third on table* C. *the center door, which he had left open, slams. He pauses, frightened, leaves this lamp partly turned down, stage dim.*] Curse the wind!

Ali [*In* PAULINE'S *chamber.*] Is that you, Pauline?

Hec [*Uneasy, whispers.*] Aline! How unfortunate.

Ali [*Same.*] Have you seen my book anywhere?

Hec What shall I do? Remain? Go? Bah! she will presently go to her own room. I will return. [*About to go* C.

Ali [*Entering, quickly.*] Why don't you answer? Hector!

Hec [*Low.*] Yes, I, Aline, I.

Ali Here, at this hour! Some accident! [*A step forward.*

Hec No.

Ali Then why—

Hec Why have I come? What shall I say to you? The day appeared so long, away from you, that this evening,—at the risk of

seeming a little extravagant,—I have profited by your little key,—
[*Movement by* ALINE.]—and I have penetrated here for the purpose of
seeing you.
Ali Only to see me?
Hec Do you doubt it?
Ali How foolish!
Hec Not very foolish. Since my dream is accomplished, I see
you—
Ali And now that you do so, we must part.
Hec Already, when I've only come?
Ali It is already too much that you have come. You make a fine
use of my key, truly. Suppose some one had seen you open that
door to-night?
Hec But no one did.
Ali And Pauline, who is in the park.
Hec [*Hesitating between the desire to go, and that of remaining.*] Ah! she
is in the Park.
Ali Yes, come, good-night.
Hec Not yet.
Ali Yes, come.   [*Opens door.*
Hec How ravishing this evening. That white robe—
Ali The door is open, you know.
Hec Only two words.
Ali Only one. Go!
Hec What cruelty! when I'm so happy as to find myself alone
with you.
Ali You will see me right away at the ball, that is enough.
Hec But *right away* does not hinder now!
Ali Just see what it is to spoil you. You are no longer reasona-
ble. It is not right for you to be here.
Hec It is not good to find ourselves alone together, enjoying one
of our old talks?
Ali I did not say it was not good, I said it was not *right*.
Hec Why not?
Ali I don't know, but it is not proper.
Hec With me?
Ali With you, above all. Oh, Hector, do go, I am afraid.
Hec Why do you fear?
Ali [*Dispirited.*] If we should be seen alone together, and you who
wish to be so secret, and who do not wish even Pauline to know—
Hec [*Quickly, taking her hand.*] Don't you know, we must arrange
our plans, as to our course in respect to her. You cannot say now,
I am not reasonable. I speak of business.
                               [*He makes her sit down gently on lounge n.*
Ali I give you five minutes. [*Taking out watch, and laying it on her
lap.*] There! five minutes.
Hec Make it ten.
Ali Five!
Hec Ten; I shan't have time to say anything.
Ali Go on then; but there's one lost already. Speak quickly, I
have my eyes on the hands.

Hec [*Sitting near her.*] I wish, then, to tell you—Oh, come, look at me a little.

Ali No! no! the business; go on.

Hec Aline!

Ali Eight minutes! Let us be serious.

Hec You will not turn your eyes a little to me?

Ali No.

Hec Oh, but yes.

Ali Oh, but no.

Hec Oh, but yes. For I will speak to you so tenderly, my look shall seek yours with so much obstinacy, and so much love, that these pretty hands [*Kissing the fingers.*] will have to keep these pretty ears from listening to me, and your heart shall not lose one of my words, one of my glances; and then the moment will come when these dear little hands will fall so gently into mine, and these rebellious eyes will have to give me the charity of a smile; when we will find ourselves at last, hand in hand, eyes in eyes, as it should be when we love; [*She turns to him gently.*] just as we are now, because we do love, Aline, we do love, in spite of you—

Ali I am a coward who has no will of her own.

Hec [*Kissing her fingers, arm round her waist.*] Because you love me, Aline, as I love you.

Ali [*Disengaging herself.*] If Pauline should come.

Hec Good heavens, let Pauline alone; who thinks of Pauline.

Ali See how seriously we talk.

Hec What is more serious than to love?

Ali [*Rising.*] Oh, I was wrong to give you that key.

Hec [*Following her.*] Again!

Ali More than ever. O, go, go, Hector, I beg you.

Hec Well, I will go. [ALINE *pleased.*] But not till you say you love me.

Ali [*Not convinced.*] Well, I love you; now go.

Hec O, say it better than that.

Ali Presently, at the ball.

Hec No, right away, now, and I will go.

Ali For sure?

Hec On my honor.

Ali Well! no, I cannot say it.

Hec Because——

Ali Because there is something in me that stops on my lips all that comes from my heart. Heaven knows that not one moment of this day has passed without your being present in my thoughts; yet, to-night there is no happiness in seeing you.

Hec Aline!

Ali O, let me tell you all. You speak so gently to me, there is another who speaks louder to me here, and which says: "Aline, he ought not to be here, and you ought not to listen to him." You shudder, you are afraid—that proves you are in fault, for one only hides for evil deeds, and trembles because he feels guilty.

Hec Aline! Guilty!

Ali Yes, yes; because what you are doing is not right, is not right!

Hec But my dear child!——

Ali No, I will not listen to you, I dare not look at you. Your words choke me, your eyes wound me. O, Hector, I never thought I should be pained at seeing you ; it is frightful, this feeling—and so strange, and I feel miserable, unhappy.   [*Falls on seat, weeping,* R.

Hec Tears !

Ali It is foolish, I know.

Hec No, it is not foolish ; forgive me, Aline, and weep no more. You are right, I ought not to be here. But the only one guilty is I, and a hundred times more guilty than you think. And you are the angel who saves me from the unworthy action I was about to commit.

Ali You ?

Hec To come here as I have to-night, for such a purpose, is most wicked and dishonest. Do not regret these tears, Aline ; I bless them, dear friend that you are, for they have made me blush for myself ; and I will go this time—yes, I will go like a thief of night, surprised by the breaking of day. Ashamed of my fault, and proud to escape it. My eyes turned to you, my duty, my truth.

Ali [*Happy.*] Ah, you are going.

Hec [*Putting key on table.*] But first this key—the accomplice of my fault—take it ! Take it, Aline, I want it no more, it burns me.

Ali Keep it till to-morrow.

Hec No, no ! to demand on my knees your hand, and with it all the happiness of my life, I will come to-morrow—but I will enter by the great door, like an honest man.

Ali To-morrow, then ?

Hec 'Till to-morrow.

Ali Now, now I love you ! [*Embraces him and he exits by* C. *and goes* L., *leaving door open.*] Ah ! I feel so happy, again. I hope he will not lose himself in the park.

[*Is following him with her eyes, when* PAULINE *comes from other direction. Both down.*

Pau Aline !

Ali [*Frightened.*] Oh !

Pau What is the matter ? you are all——

Ali Yes, I found myself alone, and was beginning to be a little afraid.

Pau Madame Boutille is waiting for you at the gate.

Ali Then kiss me. I am going to tell you something to-morrow.

Pau What is it ?

Ali Kiss me tenderly.

Pau And don't I do so every day, dear one ; come, tell me now.

Ali No, to-morrow—to-morrow.   [*Off* R. C.

Pau [*Solus.*] A confidence ! A secret ! Ah, dear little sister, yours is something that can be told. While I—I dare not think ! If that imprudent man should seek to enter the park again to-night in spite of my forbidding him ; and if he should be surprised. [*At* C. *door.*] The night is calm and cool—but I suffocate with my fears. He dare not come. He cannot. All is locked. Oh, if this could be ended ; this cursed consequence of my vanity, in listening for one instant to senseless flatteries. O, if I could be rid of the agonies of this night.

BARON enters abruptly, at L.

Bar What! still stirring, my dear.
Pau Ah! I—yes. I am taking the air.
Bar And all alone!
Pau Yes, Aline has just gone, and my women are off to the ball.
Bar Ah! I have just come from this famous ball.
Pau You danced?
Bar By the advice of Aline, I have been making popularity.
[PAULINE *starts.*] What are you looking for?
Pau [*Who has been listening at back uneasily.*] Nothing.
[*Comes forward and sits.*
Bar The air is too fresh. [*Going to close door.*
Pau No, leave it open, I beg. [*Aside.*] I was mistaken—it was the wind.
Bar You want to repose and I am chattering here. Will you go to your chamber?
Pau No, I have time enough to be smothered there.
Bar Shall I serve as your maid?
Pau [*Smiling.*] Shall I trust you?
Bar I will try and not be too bungling. We commence with the ear-rings, don't we?
Pau As you like.
Bar [*Commencing.*] Do you know you have an adorable ear?
Pau You think so!
Bar Yes, I remember when I paid court to you, I made it the object of very particular examination. [*Goes to loose the other.*] I have always had a particular taste for the feminine ear.
Pau Ah!
Bar Very few men, you know, love an entire woman all at once. Some attach themselves to the eyes, others to the hair, the mouth, the teeth—but they neglect the ear. That's wrong ; nothing is so original, so individual, so expressive as the feminine ear. A pretty ear, well designed, transparent, and pink, like this one, for instance.
Pau Ah!
Bar Ah, forgive me, I have pinched it.
Pau A little.
Bar A distraction ; where shall I put these?
Pau Give them to me, I will put them in my jewel-box.
Bar This hand! burning! You have a fever.
Pau It is nothing.
Bar What a pity I am not able to take away your pain. If I could only give you to-night a little of my good humor and my health in exchange for one of your griefs. That would be a relief to you and not a grief to me. Now, for the necklace.
[*Is about to take it, when a loud call is heard in park, answered by another and another, in distance.*

Pau [*Trembling.*] Those cries!

Bar What was that?

Pau I don't know.

Bar [*Going to door.*] It is in the park ; sounds like signals.

Pau Close the door ; I am very cold.

Bar Stay ! they are calling me.

Pau I heard nothing.

La M [*Outside.*] Baron ! Baron !

Bar I knew it. I am called.

La M [*Entering.*] Baron, quick.

Bar What is it?

La M There's a robber in the park. The villagers saw him enter and then closed up all the entrances.

Pau [*Overcome.*] It is he.

Bar Some drunkard.

Pau You are going?

Bar Do not fear. It is only some fellow escaped from the festival, and the villagers, over-anxious for me, are chasing him about. I will be back in an instant. [*She attempts to restrain him.*] Come, come, this is child's play. There, go into your chamber—lock yourself in —no one will come. [*Leads her off.*] Now then, for the robber.

[*Exit* L., *with* LA M.

Re-enter PAULINE, *nervous.*

Pau It is he. They have seen him ; they have caught him. This is the evil I felt coming. What shall I say ? [*Cries in distance.*] Ah ! Heavens, what an abyss.

Enter HECTOR, *hastily,* C.

Hec Surrounded on all sides. No way left but the house.

Pau [*Seeing him.*] Ah !

Hec Madame—a door—an escape—no matter where !

Pau There is none—none !

Hec There.

Pau My chamber.

Hec Here !

Pau Aline's ! Fly. [*Cries without.*

Hec Impossible ; they come by every road. [*Turning.*] By heaven, I will strangle the first.

Pau My husband !

Hec He ! then all is over.

Pau I am lost. Oh, sir, invent a pretext—a reason—quick. Oh ! miserable ; why did you seek me ? I fled from you. Why have you come ? You are a villain.

Hec A villain, madame ?

Pau Yes, a man who comes like you at night is but a villain—or a thief.

Hec [*As if struck by an idea.*] Ah ! true ! a thief !

Bar [*Outside.*] This way ! this way ? [HECTOR *puts out light.*

Pau [*Almost fainting.*] They are here. I am lost.

Hec No, madame. You are saved. [*Catches her as she is falling.*
Pau [*Repeating mechanically.*] Saved.
Hec [*Leading her* R. 1 E.] Yes, yes; courage and silence. I will save you. [*Exit, as* BARON, FLIBBARD, GRANCHOU, BOBOSSE, *and other villagers enter* R. *and* L. C.
Bar Guard every door!

Re-enter HECTOR, *quickly, advances, and then, as if surprised, tries to retreat again.*

All There he is. [BARON *seizes him down* L. C.
Hec In the name of heaven do not ruin me. I will give up everything. Here are your diamonds. [*Takes from his bosom the diamond necklace which was on* PAULINE's *neck.*
Bar The diamonds.
Hec Yes, from the jewel box. Have mercy, I am of good family! hide me!
Bar Miserable boy!
HECTOR *falls on lounge, hiding his face with right hand;* BARON *holds left. All come down.*
Flib [*Maliciously.*] Well, Baron?
Bar Well, you were right, gentlemen, it was a thief.
Flib and others [*As if disconcerted.*] A thief?
[PAULINE *appears above, listening.*
Bar Yes, taken in the act. [*Opens* HECTOR's *hand, and shows necklace.*]
The diamonds of the Baroness, left on her table.
Flib [*Coolly.*] Let the young man speak it himself. [*Nods to others.*
Bar [*To* HEC.] You hear!
Hec [*Slowly and with effort, averting his face.*] The Baron speaks only the truth. *I am the thief!* *Tableau. Rage of conspirators.*

ACT III.

SCENE.—*The cabinet of the* BARON. *An apartment in purple, white and gold. Door* L. 3. E., *on* R. 1 E. *a door. At back* C. *3 steps lead to a balcony—which has curtains and glass doors, and through which the moon shines. On either side* R. *and* L. *up stage, pedestals with busts or figures; a couple of handsome pictures on sides of room* R. *and* L. *Divan or lounge in* C.; *round library table with lamp and handsome shade on* R. *An easy chair near.*

HECTOR *is discovered alone on divan.*

Hec How will this end! I dare not think. I have cast myself into this abyss with closed eyes, my conscience crying to me: "Go! it is expiation for your guilty thought!" And after all, I have only done

my duty—saved an innocent woman compromised by me in spite of
her prayers. If I had reflected I might have told him—what, a lie?
that I had come for Aline! That I might have done, had I not been
seen yesterday in the park, and yesterday I had no key given me by
Aline. Fool! by that lie I should only have compromised two women to save one, and I would have served neither. And then to
have mixed with all this scandal the name of that pure child. To
stain her with a suspicion. [*Clock strikes two.*] Two o'clock! [*Rises and
goes to window.*] Day is yet distant, and if it were not for these damned
villagers I would yet fly. The window is not far from the ground,
but they are all below there. [*Looks cautiously out.*] In arms, too!
They will not stir till they have given me up to justice. [*Seats himself.*]
What will be done with me? Taken away to prison, without doubt.
Am I not a thief? Ah! [*Sighs.*] But I must not falter. I must accuse myself—and without reserve, and more eagerly than other crim-
inals defend themselves. [*The door opens at* L. 3. E., *and the* BARON
appears with LA MARIOTTE, *who carries a tray.*] It is he! come, coolness,
confidence!

Bar There, on that table.

La M [*Putting down tray—aside.*] What a handsome young man; I
don't believe he's a thief; those sort of young men don't steal diamonds—they steal hearts! [*Aloud.*] Anything else, sir?

Bar No.

La M [*Going.*] Such a good-looking malefactor! I wish I was a
policeman and had charge of him.   [*Exit.*

Bar [*Touching* HECTOR *on shoulder.*] Come, take a glass of wine and
a biscuit; you want all your strength.

Hec I thank you, sir, I need nothing.

Bar Oh, come, come; you mustn't be starved.

Hec [*Refusing.*] Thanks, sir.   [*Turning away.*

Bar [*Gazing at him—to himself.*] Curious fellow, this. Very curious.
Good address. Good bearing. [*Aloud.*] Come, then, while we are
waiting for the Commissary of Police, whom they have gone to
fetch, suppose we talk a little about this affair of yours. I am mayor
of the place, and consequently, in the exercise of my functions, suppose I make you submit preliminarily to a little interrogation. Sit
down face to face with me.

Hec A thousand thanks—I——

Bar Yes, yes—sit down. Come, I have not a very ferocious air,
have I? Well, answer me openly. Freedom of speech at times is,
next to freedom of body, the greatest comfort. How old are you?

Hec Twenty-three years, sir.

Bar Ah! the glorious age. And see what you are making of it.
Bad, bad. Your name?

Hec Hector.

Bar The other?

Hec Sir, do not ask me. I have fallen very low, but I have hon-
orable parents; and before I would drag their name down to my
level——

Bar It is just. Then you have neither bad example nor bad train-
ing for an excuse?

Hec Neither.

Bar Then you are the more guilty. What could have been your motive?

Hec Ah, sir—temptations, desperate circumstances!

Bar Be more precise—hem! you have vices?

Ah, sir! at my age—

Bar See where they lead! To scaling walls at night—I suppose you scaled my walls, did you not? [HECTOR *bows*.] What did you hope to get in my house?

Hec [*With an effort*.] Sir, I quitted Paris yesterday in a frightful state of mind—dishonored to-morrow, in default of a certain sum of money, which I could not raise; threatened with prison—not daring to write the truth to my parents——

Bar Who live in the country, eh! [HECTOR *bows*.] And you are, I suppose, in some commercial house?

Hec [*Eagerly*.] Commercial house! yes, sir, a clerk.

Bar And you have violated the confidence of your employers?

Hec For the first time—

Bar Exactly. And now I'd bet—I'd bet it was gambling. [HECTOR *turns away*.] Well, and then—what were you going to say?

Hec [*Another effort*.] Then, sir, I came to this village. Fatality made me hear, by chance, among the crowd at the festival, accounts of the riches of your house, the jewels, the diamonds of the baroness.

Bar That animal, Flibbard, with his speeches. He'll have all the burglars in the country on my back.

Hec Then I thought—if I wait till night, the Baron will be at the ball, the servants will have gone out,—I entered the park, all the windows were open, once in, the first jewel, or jewels that I saw—
[*Respires.*

Bar Well planned; but, once possessed of the diamonds, what did you intend to do?

Hec Ah! sir, I had not asked myself that. Fancy a desperate man,—reason, hope, fear, all gone. He seizes even at guilt for safety, and it is only after the miserable deed, that he says to himself, [*With emotion*.] as I have said but now, "What have I done? For the safety of the moment, compromised my whole life!"

Bar [*Aside*.] All that has a very natural air. [*Aloud*.] Let us see. [*Nearing him*.] Perhaps you are not so culpable indeed. At twenty-three, bad companions, evil counsels, above all, accomplices—

Hec No, sir, I have not that excuse, even.

Bar You came here alone?

Hec Alone.

Bar Ah, I will wager that you do not speak all the truth, and that in your case there is another guilty person.

Hec Another!

Bar Yes, a woman!

Hec [*Starting*.] A woman!

Bar Why not? At your age, it is a very good thing, or it is a very bad thing to go after the women. Come, now, there is a woman—eh?

Hec [*Uneasily.*] I declare to you—

Bar Now don't fib about it. You have betrayed yourself, for you are even now trembling,—not for yourself, but for her. Who is she? Some baggage, eh?

Hec No, sir! No, sir!

Bar Then some young girl you have run away with, or some married woman—Hum! [HECTOR *hides his face, without answering.* BARON *watching him closely.*] A married woman, that's clear. Your shame betrays you. [*Rising.*] Well, well! Raise your son in the principles of honor and virtue, be always tender and devoted, bleed for him at every pore, and yet, for all that, he drags probity, honor, future, at the feet of the first woman who crosses his path.

Hec [*To himself, sadly.*] It is true.

Bar Your tears, poor father, your tears, despairing mother! no one thinks of that. Now, I'll wager *you* did not!

Hec Ah, my poor father! No, I did not think of him.

Bar And yet you love him?

Hec [*Leans his face in his hands.*] Have pity, sir. What avails it now, to recall all this?

Bar [*Touched, himself.*] Tears! and real ones. [HECTOR *rises, troubled.*] Come, sit down ; you tremble. [HECTOR *falls again into seat.*] Well, he has some good in him yet ; some heart. This is no feigned sorrow ; there is some stuff for an honest man. Come, now, the evil is done. No use to grieve about that ; let us think of the remedy. Have you any idea of what you must do?

Hec [*With despair.*] None!

Bar Well, then, I am more sagacious than you, because I have thought of something. It is a little risky, but as there is only one chance, we must take it or leave it. Now, my opinion is, that it would be extremely foolish for you to wait here for the Commissary of Police, and before he comes you ought to leave. [HECTOR *regards him with surprise.*] Yes, take to your legs.

Hec And you would—

Bar Yes, I might even assist you.

Hec Oh, sir, I shall owe you—

Bar Try and remain calm.

Hec Oh, sir, if you knew! I feel that it is only necessary to see our faults face to face, as I see them now, to understand how much they ought to be condemned.

Bar And it is because you appear to appreciate them at their just value, that I sentence you to repair them by future good conduct. Is it a bargain?

Hec Ah, sir!

Bar Only take care ; the first condition—

Hec Is—

Bar That you renounce the woman who has caused all the trouble.

Hec It is done, sir. The lesson was severe enough already, and your goodness completes it.

Bar And now let us think of escape.

Enter LA MARIOTTE, *with a card.*

La M The gentleman is below, sir.
Hec The Commissary, already!
La M No, sir; it is Mr. Macaire.
Hec [*Aside.*] My father!   [*Uneasy.*
Bar Show him in.   [LA M. *exits.*
Hec [*Troubled.*] Here!
Bar [*Opening door at* R.] Go in my library, and have a little patience. I will make it all right.
Hec Fatality! what brings him here?   [*Exit.*
Bar He comes just in time; he can aid me, perhaps. [MACAIRE *enters with valise, dejected and overcome.*] Why, what's the matter?
Mac Oh! the demons! Those accursed villagers!
Bar [*Laughing.*] What have they done to you?
Mac First set fire to my piazza, with their damned fireworks, and then deluged every room in my house, on the plea of preventing a conflagration; every bed is soaked with their accursed engines; everything is inundated by that fiend, Granchou, and his safety hose. My floor swims, my pictures swim, my chairs swim. Ah, my dear friend, what fatal idea impelled you to give them an engine and a half-inch butt?
Bar It was unfortunate, but you are safe.
Mac Yes; on the advice of an honest fellow, who glided up to me, saying, "Go to the Mayor, he will give you a dry bed," I have come, supported even to your door by this honest fellow.
Bar Who was it?
Mac Flibbard.
Bar Ah! there's something beneath this.
Mac Eh?
Bar Never mind. Sit down, you are welcome, and for the sake of distraction you may do me a service.
Mac To be sure.
Bar It is to play a trick on these villagers.
Mac I'll do it; what is it?
Bar Just now there entered my park, a thief.
Mac Some scoundrelly villagers.
Bar No, he is a Parisian. I believe the poor devil repentant, and I wish to give him his liberty; but how? I can't go to the Commissary,—who will arrive in a few moments,—and say, "The thief! Ah! yes, I have thanked him, and let him go." While you—now see—I confide this boy to you a moment, you watch badly, he escapes. Is it done?
Mac Lord! I wish I could collect in this chamber all the malefactors of every country in the world, and I would let them loose on the village, like a cloud of locusts.
Bar Good! Half a dozen of the villagers are below, as sentinels, armed. I will get them into my office, and when they once get tumbler in hand—
Mac [*Laughing.*] Good! Where is the thief?
Bar [*Points.*] Sh! he is in the library. Now, then, to have these

fellows round the bottle. I will go out, they will come in, you will
open the cage, and the bird is free.   [*Exit.*
Mac I will let him out with pleasure. Not being a Bouseyite, I
hope he will make them pay when he gets off. [HECTOR *has come out
softly. After assuring himself the* BARON *is gone, comes down on tip-toe, and
appears before* MACAIRE.] Hector ! !
Hec [*Closing his mouth.* [Silence ! I beg of you.
Mac But this—this thief ?
Hec It is I. But you know it is false, that there is a mistake, a
secret—a secret which I beg you to keep for the honor of a woman.
Mac But how ? Tell me !
Hec I was surprised in the room of the Baroness ; forgive me !
Tell me you forgive me. I am unfortunate only—not guilty. Do
not overwhelm me by your anger.
Mac [*Falling to seat.*] Oh, unhappy boy ! what shame.
Hec [*Putting his arms round him.*] Come ! let us not grieve—a little
firmness. We have need of all our firmness. You are listening to
me, are you not ?
Mac Oh, yes ! yes !
Hec These rascally peasants detected and pursued me—you under-
stand ; then the Baron surprised me in his wife's room.. What was
I to do—avow the truth—a crime, an infamy ? The woman was
guiltless and imperiled by my imprudence ; she was distracted, and
cried, " He will kill me ! " and as the idea struck me, I seized her
diamonds, and said to the husband, " Come, arrest me ; I am
a thief ! "
Mac But that's what I won't have said ; that my son—my
Hector, of whom I am so proud, my dear boy to be called a
thief—a stealer of diamonds ; dishonored for life ! Never ! never !
never !
Hec But I beg of you, be calm.
Mac [*Rises.*] There's no calmness ; you are not a thief. I won't
have you pass for one ; I will do my duty as a father—you have
done yours as a man. You cannot tell the truth to this husband ;
that's plain, I can, and I will.   [*Going* L.
Hec [*Interposing.*] Father !
Mac I will soften, I will extenuate, I will call you headstrong ;
say his wife knew nothing ! But what difference does it make ? let
him take it as he will. What is it to me, after all ?
Hec You are decided ? you want me to call him ?
Mac Right away.
Hec I shall. But remember, the end of all this will *then* not be a
prison, but a duel.
Mac [*Hesitating.*] A duel ! you will fight.
Hec We will fight, and I shall not have the courage to defend my-
self against this noble man whom I have outraged and who has so
generously saved me ; and if he kill me, you will have done the
deed.
Mac Kill you ! On every side shame or death ! Bah, it is child's-
play, and you only wish to scare me. You will not fight.

Hec That depends on him. If you wish to risk it——
                                    [*Goes to door.*

Mac Stop!
Hec Decide quickly.
Mac What shall I do?   [*Falls on seat.*
Hec The simplest thing in the world; keep silent and continue as I have begun; sustain my falsehood. After all, what difference does it make if I pass five minutes longer for what they think me? After that is only flight, liberty, safety.
Mac It is true!
Hec We will leave this place forever; we will never see again this man, nor his family, [*With emotion.*] nor Aline! And you know not all that I shall lose. [*Aside.*] My happiness within my grasp, and lost forever. Poor Aline!
Mac How?
Hec Let us not speak of that. He comes! You undestand; say as I do. You do not know me; I am but a criminal whom you help to save. Then in an hour, Paris; we two will be re-united, happy. You will promise—for your Hector, your boy! You don't want him to kill your boy; come! won't you say as I say?
Mac I will say anything.
Hec [*Drying his father's eyes.*] He comes! your eyes! courage, and I am saved.

BARON *entering,* L

Bar They are drinking. Quick.
Hec I am ready.
Bar Are you the man to leap from the balcony into the garden?
Mac Leap!
Hec [*Quickly.*] Oh! I believe you.
Mac Baron, you are sure.
Bar What!   [HECTOR *opens window.*
Mac Hector! Hector! take care.
Bar Hector! [*He looks at both.* HECTOR *half over, hesitates. Silence!*] Hector! you know him, then.
Mac [*Stammering.*] Yes—I—
Bar [*Suddenly, after a pause.*] Your son! [*Both silent.*] Answer me
Mac Alas, yes! My son.
Bar [*To* HECTOR, *who returns.*] You did not tell me that.
Hec You permitted me to keep silent as to my name.
Bar True! But silence on that point did not authorize you to falsify on others. [*To* MACAIRE.] You told me this morning your son was a lawyer.
Mac Yes.
Bar He told me that he was a clerk in a commercial house.
Hec Pardon me, sir; I spoke falsely.
Bar When I appealed to your frankness. When I questioned you as a friend—as a father.
Hec [*Embarrassed.*] I trembled for my father, sir, and the better to divert suspicion—
Bar But then this tale--money embezzled—a falsehood! All that

which justified, or at least explained your fault, your remorse, your
tears which touched me, falsehoods, too, like all the rest.
  Hec Oh! sir, do you doubt?
  Bar Your tears, no! but your remorse, yes!
  Mac [*Anxiously.*] Sir, time presses.
  Bar [*Closing window.*] Pardon me, nothing presses.
  Mac And the liberty you were about to give him——
  Bar Was the unhappy penitent, not the hardened criminal, who
by hypocritical tears stole my pity.
  Mic Ah, sir, if not for him, for me. I pray you—I am his father
—his dishonor is mine. I have done nothing to you, I am not
guilty, and it is I that you strike first.
  Bar For your sake, then. [*Goes to window. Opens it. Listens.*]
Bah! let him escape now if he can.   [*Murmurs without.*
  Mac O, thanks, sir.
  Hec [*Over balcony.*] At last!
  Flib [*In garden.*] There he is.   [*Gun shot.*
  All There he is!
  Bar Too late.
  Mac They are there!
  Hec All!
  Gran [*Appears above balcony, shouting.*] Here's the Commissary of
Police.

                     Enter LA MARIOTTE, L.

  La M The Commissary of Police is here, sir.
  Bar It was ordained!   Poor father!
[*Goes up. Doors open L. COMMISSARY appears, followed by his secretary.*
      FLIBBARD, BOBOSSE, PIPARTE, *and* VILLAGERS *enter.*
Mr. Commissary, I beg—
  Com A thief, they tell me, M. Baron.
[FLIBBARD *with officiousness clears table for* SECRETARY. COMMISSARY
            sits L. FLIB. *prepares pens, paper, &c.*
  Bar Nothing more, fortunately. This young man, I'm sorry to
say—
  Com You demand his arrest!
  Bar Yes.
          [FLIBBARD *exchanges glances with peasants, who arrange at back.*
  Com Will you have the goodness to give us in a few words, an ac-
count of what has taken place.
  Bar It is very easy. I surprised this gentleman in the saloon on
the first floor, at the moment he was trying to escape with the dia-
monds of the Baroness. [*Handing them over.*]
  Com [*Taking diamonds.*] Ah! in flagrante delictu?
  Bar Yes, in the act.
  Com Does the accused admit the exactness of this statement?
I do, sir.
  Com [*Surprised.*] So! Think well of your own interest, the gravity
of your answers. You came with deliberate intent—with intent to
steal—these diamonds?

Hec To steal these diamonds—yes, sir.
Com Take it down.
Mac [*About to rise.*] No, no—I——
Hec [*Forcing him down.*] I will make him kill me, I warn you.
                                    [*This unnoticed by others.*
Com Prisoner, your name
Hec Hector Macaire.
Com Profession?
Hec Lawyer.   [*Movement of surprise.*]
Com Residence?
Hec In this village, with my father.
   [*Shows his father, at the same time pressing his hand affectionately.*
Com What motive prompted you to so condemnable an action?
Hec Gambling, sir. I lost at play. My father, losing all patience,
refused me aid; and then—
Bar Pardon me, Mr. Commissary—but there is such a discrepancy
between this statement and what his father told me, that I beg you
to allow me—   [*Rising.*
Com Certainly, Baron.
Bar Mr. Macaire, pardon my intruding on your grief by my ques-
tions.
Hec [*Quickly—aside.*] Say as I do Courage!
Bar Your son is then a gambler?
Mac [*With an effort.*] Yes.
Bar How, then, did you tell me this very morning that he was
such an excellent son?
       [*MACAIRE is about to speak, but is interrupted by HECTOR.*
Hec [*Quickly.*] My father believed I had reformed.
Bar I am speaking to your father. You were so proud of your
son—so glad of his return—how do you reconcile all this?
Hec My father would not betray my faults, sir, you see. He would
not tell you the truth. It is this: that, for the last three years
there have been no faults I have not committed, and no sorrows that
I have not made him feel. Is it not so, father? [*Taking his hand.*]
Twenty times he has had to pay my debts, and conceal my follies.
Is it not true, father? Say the truth then, since I avow it—say as
I do.
Mac [*With effort.*] It is true.
Hec [*Triumphant.*] You see.
Bar I see very well that Mr. Macaire is pained to overwhelm you
with his testimony, and I understand why; but what I do not un-
derstand is the eagerness you exhibit in accusing yourself so strongly.
Hec [*Troubled.*] It is that I may repair by this frankness all the
falsehoods I have been guilty of towards you.
Bar [*Aside.*] There is something under all this which I do not see.
Com Since the accused confesses, my task is ended, and all may
retire.
Hec [*Respiring.*] It is over.
Fhb Pardon me, Mr. Commisary, but the witnesses.
Com The crime is acknowledged—the rest is with the court.
Fhb [*Meaningly.*] Excuse me; but the declaration of a witness may

enlighten the case from another point. I demand that the witnesses shall be heard.

Com Very well! quick, then, are they present?

La M They are, sir.

Flib All except the Baroness!

Bar La Mariotte—the Baroness.

Flib Now for it. [*To others.*] Watch me now.

Hec [*Aside.*] Again.

Enter PAULINE, *with* LA M.

Com Pardon us, madame, this indispensable formality. In five minutes I will give you back to your slumber in peace.

BARONESS *sits* L., *near* BARON.

Flib Now, then ; some one saw the accused introduce himself into the park.

Gran, Pip, and Bob Yes, Mr. Flibbard.

Com Who first?

Pip I, Mr. Commissary—I saw him open the green gate.

Bar He entered by the green gate.

Pip With a key.

Bar With a key.

Hec [*Quickly.*] Yes, sir, a false key.

Bar You said you scaled the walls!

Hec It was a falsehood.

Bar Another!

Bob I saw him first!

Pip No, I did.

Gran [*Importantly,* L. C.] Both wrong. Who saw the young man first? I did?

Com You?

Gran They saw him enter to-day—I saw him enter yesterday.

Flib [*Emphatically.*] Yesterday! [*Movement of all.*

Bar Yesterday! [*Quickly, in hoarse voice, clutching* GRANCHOU'S *arm.*] You saw this young man yesterday in my park?

Gran As plainly as I see you, though it was dark

Bar It was night?

Gran On the stroke of eleven.

Bar Are you sure?

Gran Sure? Well, seeing that I have still at home his hat, which he lost, and he knows it well, the rascal—

Bar [*To* HECTOR.] Then you entered my park last night?

Hec Yes.

Bar [*With cold anger, that warms, and which he seeks to restrain.*] So, then all that you have told me is but a frightful tissue of lies. Why were you in my house? For what purpose? Speak!

Hec To plan here, what I did to-day

Bar The theft of the diamonds?

Hec Yes.

Bar How could you know yesterday that they existed, since the Baroness wore them to-night for the first time?

Hec I did not come for diamonds only. I hoped to find gold, jewels.

Bar At eleven at night, in a habited mansion, when everything was lit up, and the domestics were about.

Hec Exactly. I renounced my purpose then, and fled.

Gran [*With assumed innocence.*] Yes! He ran away when the Baroness went into the house.

Bar [*After this stroke, runs to seize* GRANCHOU *by the throat, then stops.*] Mr. Commissary, I ask you to dismiss every one. I have need of all my coolness.

Fib [*Taking* GRANCHOU'S *arm, as all go out.*] It tells.
[BAR., COM., HEC., *and* MAC. *remain.*

Bar [*After leading* BARONESS *out, and closing door.*] Then, having fled last night for some reason, you came again to-night.

Hec Yes.

Bar And you were seen, and pursued.

Hec [*Emphasizing.*] And then, only, I took refuge in the house, not knowing that the apartment I entered was that of the Baroness.

Bar Yes, and knowing that you are pursued, you take the diamonds, in order that you may be arrested with your hands full.

Hec I still hoped to fly with my booty. I was alone. The necklace sparkled so on the table.

Bar And why did you leave the ear-rings?

Hec They were not there.

Bar I beg your pardon, I saw the Baroness put them in the box.

Hec I only saw the necklace.

Bar Which was not there, for now that I remember, when I went out, the Baroness had it still on her neck.

Hec Nevertheless, I took it from the box, where it could only have been placed by the Baroness.

Bar [*Going to door, and calling.*] Pauline! [BARONESS *enters.*] Why did you take your necklace off at the moment they cried out in the park, "A thief!"

Pau [*Troubled.*] But I did not, I kept it on.

Bar [*To* HECTOR.] Ah! [*To* PAULINE.] It was not then in the jewel box?

Hec [*Aside.*] The unfortunate! [*Aloud.*] No, it is true, the Baroness had it on, still.

Bar [*Raging.*] Ah! but then! you were not alone. You were with her! And all that I have heard is a lie, from first to last.

Com Baron!

Bar Oh, let me be! I want the truth. I want it, and I will have it. How did you get this necklace? Answer! I want to know.

Hec Well, I did not wish to avow it, because it makes my crime more grave. I tore it from her neck.

Bar [*Turning to his wife.*] And she let you do so without calling for help.

Hec She was icy with fear.

Pau [*Losing caution.*] Yes, and in my distress, fearing your voice, and fearing you were about to return —

Bar You fied! [*Silence.* PAULINE, *broken down, drops on chair.* MA-
CAIRE *crosses between his son and the* BARON, *to protect former.*] Mr. Ma-
caire, have you anything to say to me in defense of your son?
Mac [*Frightened at his look.*] Nothing, sir.
Bar It is necessary, then, to arrest him, like a miserable thief
and reprobate as he is. [MACAIRE *makes a gesture of mercy.*] Neverthe-
less, if you assure me that he has not lied at every point, that it
was really to save a woman compromised by him—
Mac I do not say that—
Bar Why not, if it be true?
Mac But it is not! No one says so.
Bar [*Aside.*] Well, the father will not speak, the other must be
made to. [*To* COMMISSARY.] Mr. Commissary, [*Indicating* MACAIRE.]
this man is a false witness; he is an accomplice, arrest the father.
Hec [*Starting before* MACAIRE.] My father— •
Bar The two are thieves together.
Hec A thief! You! He!
Mac [*Seeking to calm him.*] Let him go on.
Hec Arrest you! A prison! Never!
Mac [*Trying to stop him.*] Silence! Silence!
Hec Let him kill me if he wishes, but he shall not make you the
victim of a theft I have not committed.
Bar [*Bursting out.*] Good! That is what I wished to get at. [*He
turns and sees* PAULINE *fall as a corpse. She has fallen from her chair to her
knees. He recoils a step. Then in an undertone to her.*] These are the
blows that no man expects, and when we meet them, where is our
refuge? [*Sorrowfully.*] Ah! what have I done to merit this?
Com Baron, the people outside.
Bar True! [*Composes his face, raises her to chair, dries his eyes, and
opens door where villagers are.*] Enter! Enter! [*All come in.* FLIBDARD,
GRANCHOU *forward.*] All is over. The young man admits, and, by
my faith, liking his frankness, Mr. Commissary, I withdraw my
complaint.
Flib What! You let him go?
Bar Yes; he is so young, a good lesson will suffice. [*Taking the
arm of his wife.*] Let us go in, you are heavy with sleep. Come, to
bed! [*As he crosses and passes* HECTOR.] You will wait for me, sir!
Good night, gentlemen.
Gran [*Stupefied.*] I don't understand.
Flib Our first hit is a miss.   [*Curtain.*

ACT IV.

SCENE.—*Same as Second Act. Against the left wall, a desk and chair.
All very dark beyond in the park.*

LA MARIOTTE *enters with a lighted lamp with shade, which she places on table.
The* BARON *and* PAULINE *follow.*

Bar [*Affecting nonchalance, to* LA MARIOTTE.] Has everybody left the
house, Mariotte?   [BARONESS *sits, R. C.*

La M Yes, sir, there is no one but Mr. Hector and his father—who are in the park. The father wanted to lead him away, but Mr. Hector said that he was waiting for your orders.

Bar [*Carelessly.*] What o'clock is it?

La M Three o'clock, sir.

Bar Ah, day is not far off. Aline has not come home from the ball.

La M No, sir, but it will be soon over.

Bar That's well! [*To* PAULINE.] You need nothing, Madame. No! [*To* LA MARIOTTE.] You may go.

La M [*Going*] The Commissary has gone off and the young man is not locked ; this is the way they treat thieves, and then wonder that the papers say "crime is on the increase." I think I'd better look after the handsome young robber myself. [*Exit,* L.

Bar [*Whose face changes as soon as* LA MARIOTTE *goes out.*] Now, Madame, I am ready to listen to you. [*Sits,* L.

Pau [*With effort, rising,* C.] I have nothing to say; everything accuses me, and what I might utter in my defense, you would not believe.

Bar That is to say, this young man is not your lover?

Pau [*Quickly.*] No, he is not! [*She checks herself at the sight of his ironical smile.*] But you see—— [*As if despairing to convince him.*

Bar Well, at all events, let us know on what you base your claim to be considered innocent.

Pau I am not altogether innocent. I have committed a fault that I shall atone for with the happiness of my whole life. I was giddy and foolish, and during the voyage that I made with Aline, I did repulse at once, those protestations of love, which I ought not to have even listened to. But while there is that which condemns me, there is also that which absolves me. I saw my peril in time to avoid it by an abrupt departure. But after two months he came again : he begged me to grant him an interview. What could I do? I thought that if I appealed to his honor he would forbear his persecution. And then, he had letters of mine ; you see I tell you everything! Letters which you may read, sir, but which I did not desire to leave in his hands ; and therefore it was necessary to see him, and to see him I had to go to the park—at night. And day before yesterday I opened to him the little gate of the garden. Yes, it is true, I opened it, and I acknowledge it.

Bar Go on.

Pau It was one fault more. I know it too well, now, but I was mad with terror. He came, and all that could be done to repair a fault I did. I prayed, I supplicated, I wept. He refused to obey me, and to depart—or to give me my letters. I said to him : "You are a villain, and I hate you ;" and I swear to you I spoke truly. [*Looking at him.*] You do not believe me yet?

Bar No ; because you have not explained to me, why, after being repulsed by you the day before yesterday, he came again last night.

Pau [*Excited.*] It was against my will—in spite of me.

Bar And how did he enter the park by the same little gate, if he had not received from you a key to facilitate this second rendezvous?

Pau From me—a key! a rendezvous!

Bar Apparently, since he was seen to open that gate.

Pau But I protest, I know nothing about that. It was not I—that is all I can say; But think, how could I have been awaiting him? I was here with you—here when they came crying: "There is a robber in the park."

Bar Yes, and then your countenance changed.

Pau Because I said to myself, "It must be he."

Bar [*Quickly.*] So then you did expect him?

Pau [*Wounded.*] Ah! after all I have told you. Accuse me, I answer no more.

Bar I do not accuse you—

Pau [*On her knees.*] Well, kill me! I prefer death to all the tortures I foresee.

Bar [*Rises, c.*] For you there is neither death nor torture. Death is for another, and the torture is for me, alone. [PAULINE *rises.*] You have no need to defend yourself; there is some one who pleads your cause better than you! It is I. Twice just now a blood-red veil passed across my sight, and the hand which sustained your steps grew cruel! But I tamed the violence of a second, for I said to myself: "If there be a crime, it is not she who was the first guilty—but you!"

Pau You!

Bar Guilty—because, at an age when one can no longer inspire love, I committed the unpardonable fault of uniting your life to mine. I, almost an old man—you in the springtime of a happy girlhood; but I loved you dearly, and I did not know then that it is with such love that at my age men make themselves hateful. [*Movement of* PAULINE. *He continues without regarding it.*] I said to myself, "I will be so good, so tender, so constantly affectionate! I will make myself so young to please her, that in default of love she will show at least some gratitude—and honor doing the rest we will both be safe. I am deceived; but it was not necessary to punish me so cruelly. I forgive you; I have against you neither anger nor desire of vengeance. And the only thing which I cannot tear out is a pitiful sorrow, that I ought to overcome, but cannot.

Pau Oh, sir! I beg you—for our common happiness—listen to me, and believe me.

Bar I cannot. If you desire it, we will see later what ought to be decided upon for our common good. For the present I desire to be alone, and if you will go to your chamber—   [*He opens the door.*

Pau Yes!

[BARON *goes to his desk, which he opens. He turns and sees* PAULINE *still there.*

Bar I have opened the door, madame, why do you wait?

Pau [*Supporting herself against back of arm-chair.*] I wait till I have strength.

Bar [*Is about to give his arm, then hesitates.*] I will call your maid.

Pau I will go alone.

[*Going feebly. The* BARON *from back makes a step after, then stops. She exits,* R. 1 E.

Bar [*Alone*] It is such a sight as that makes men kill without pity. Miserable wretch! A drop of his blood for every tear.

[*Rising and going towards* L.

Enter HECTOR, *quickly.*

It is well, sir, you are in haste, so am I. [HECTOR *is looking round for* PAULINE.] But we cannot fight before daylight. It will soon be drawn. Here are the weapons. [*Opening desk.*

Hec [*Pale and anxious.*] Sir, a single word; the Baroness—she has told you—has she not? It is not a demand which I make, but a prayer.

Bar Well!

Hec She has convinced you that there is but one guilty person—myself. She has told you so, and you believe it?

Bar No!

Hec You do not believe that she is innocent.

Bar I do not recognize in you, either the right or the power to convince me.

Hec So, because by a fatality I have met in my path an honest woman to persecute with my foolish love—because I have been bad enough to come even into your house to renew my odious pursuit—because those people cut off my retreat at the moment I was about to leave without having seen her—because of *my* follies, my *crimes*, you will make this unfortunate woman bear your anger as well as my persecution.

Bar Have done, sir! Daylight is approaching.

Hec How can I attest my truth—her honor! what heaven! what God! what oath!

Bar None! Why should I believe you, since I have not believed her?

Hec [*Overcome.*] It is true, sir; but will no proof, nothing?—

Bar Again! you weary me.

Hec [*Hopeful.*] Ah, yes—her letters. [*Taking them from his pocket.*] See, sir—two letters—which she would have reclaimed. Read, sir, they are the clearest proof her innocence.

Bar [*Taking them coolly.*] It is her writing.

Hec Yes, yes; read, sir!

Bar Why should I? You give me to read what cannot be read. [*Tears them up.*] Is that all? what else have you to offer me?

Hec [*Coldly and resolutely, after a silence.*] My life!

Bar [*Sardonically.*] At last; here is your pistol and ammunition. You will load, yourself.

Hec As you please.

Bar You will go into the park.

Hec My father is there, anxious and on the watch. How shall we avoid him?

Bar [*Indicating* L. 1 E.] Cross that chamber; at the bottom is a little door, it opens on a path which leads to the extremity of the park.

Hec It is well.

Bar Follow the stream, and you will come upon a deserted place, where we shall be undisturbed. You have a quarter of an hour to get there ; it will then be daylight. I will leave here ten minutes after you. Get into ambush where you will—for the first who sees the other will shoot—like the Indians. Are you content?

Hec Yes.

Bar Witnesses are useless ! Besides, we should not find any to assent to these conditions ; and if you will, be punctual.

Hec I shall be there—

Bar [*Turning away.*] Then I will detain you no longer.

Hec Pardon me, 1 have a word—to write.

Bar [*Designating desk with materials.*] Do it.

Hec [*Writing.*] Will you be good enough to charge yourself with the delivery of this to its address, in case—

Bar I promise.

Hec Thanks !   [*Folds letter and leaves it on table.*

Bar In ten minutes—

Hec In ten minutes, sir, I swear to you, you will find me.
                                    [*Exit,* R. 2 E.

[*Daybreak at back.* BARON *takes up pistol and begins to examine it.* ALINE *appears at* C., *frightened by the rising sun, and dismissing her maid at the door.*

Ali I shan't want you now. Why, Baron, are you up and about already ?

Bar [*Hiding pistol behind him.*] Aline, child, is that you? Good morning.

Ali [*Taking off hat, veil, gloves,* &c.] Oh, dear, I have danced with all the village, and only left off when the musicians cried, "Mercy," what have you got there ?

Bar Me ?

Ali A pistol ; what is that for !

Bar Nothing ; I was about to take the morning air in the park— and if I meet a rabbit—

Ali [*Laughing.*] Hunt rabbits with a pistol—why don't you take a pen-knife ?

Bar [*Looking at his watch.*] It is less troublesome than a gun.

Ali You'll never kill anything with that ; mark my words.

Bar Be it so—we shall see.

Ali Well, it's your business, not mine. [*Falling into seat,* C.] Lord, how I have danced. [*Hums an air, and drums with her toes on the floor.*

Bar [*Taking his hat.*] You must go to bed.

Ali No, indeed ! I have a great mind to take a walk in the park with you.

Bar What ! in your ball dress ?

Ali Oh! I shan't wear it again ; and the walk would be so nice.
                                    [*Rising.*

Bar [*Quickly.*] No, no ; go to bed—you are ready to drop with fatigue.

Ali [*Taking his arm, and detaining him.*] And if I am, it was all for your sake—and you don't even thank me ! Ungrateful !

Bar For my sake ! [*Absently looks at his watch.*

Ali What is the matter with you ?—you are always looking at your watch.

Bar Me ! Nothing.

Ali Put down your blunderbuss, and let me hear your thanks for the solid support I have given to your municipal power this glorious night.

Bar [*Absently and nervous.*] How so ?

Ali By dancing you into popularity ! You see, in the first place, I would have none but the villagers for my partners, and that tickled them immensely ; besides, I taught them some new steps. First. there was Mr. Cassegraine, he is a grocer, and was perfumed with coffee. I waltzed with him, and as we went round, I looked reproachfully into his green eyes, and said to him, "Why do you hate the Baron, who is so good to you ?" and then he said—he was very short of breath, and his words jumped out like rabbits at every step. [*Imitating.*] "Me, miss? I don't hate—him ! It's—that—rascal Chipoteau !—not me !" Then it came to be Chipoteau's turn. He is a romantic mason and builder. I was very sentimental with him—we had a Danish polka. I said to him, "You are naughty to be an enemy of my brother !" he blurted out—you know the Danish is not a very good measure to talk in, and it was very funny. [*Imitating.*] "Oh—not—I—miss ! It's—that—conceited Loubat over there !" Good ! In the next Lanciers I balanced to corners where my friend Loubat was, and attacked him. [*Imitating.*] Never, miss ! the Baron ! I love him ! He's a man among men !" And so I went through with them all. It was a High Political Ball, and when daylight came I had forty sworn friends—the flower of the Bouscyites, who, if I had said "Which of you will pull Mr. Flibbard's ears for me ?" would have shouted in a chorus, " All of us ! every man !"

[*Falls on chair laughing. During this scene she dances at times in imitation of her own manner when talking, and then in imitation of her awkward partners. Always dancing to the* BARON *when she represents her own manner.*

Bar [*Tapping her chin.*] You are a perfect little diplomatist.
[*Looks at his watch, and tries to get away.*

Ali Oh, but see now, it is not right to accept my services that way, and then run off.

Bar I know, my child—but the hour, the hour.

Ali Never mind the hour, the most particular business now is—my reward !

Bar Quickly, then ! what do you wish ?

Ali Don't say it that way. [*Lowering her voice.*] Are we alone ?

Bar Yes.

Ali Well, then, another would have asked to be allowed to share your power, I am more modest—I only ask your assistance.

Bar For what?

Ali [*Lowering her voice.*] To be married.

Bar Ah, that's too long a story! a little later!

Ali Well, as you please—but I'm determined not to leave you.

Bar [*Trying to get away.*] Come, come, my dear child—

Ali I'll cling to you, and I'll follow you into the park—there now.

Bar Three words, then—quick.

Ali No, six—he loves me; I love him.

Bar Well, what then?

Ali What then? was there ever? I'll tell you. He's going to demand of you my hand, this very afternoon! And you will consent?

Bar It is agreed.

Ali You can't say "it's agreed," because you don't know him.

Bar The moment he pleases you—

Ali Oh, as for that, he will please you, too. He is a charming young man, whom Pauline and I met, on our trip to the Pyrenees.

Bar [*Stopping.*] Ah!

Ali And who turns out to be the son of our neighbor.

Bar [*Quickly.*] Macaire!

Ali Yes, Hector!

Bar And he loves you! He has told you so—he has promised to ask for your hand?

Ali Yes, we made it all up in advance.

Bar She too! The villain!   [*Takes up pistol.*

Ali Well, what's the matter?—you don't listen to me.

Bar [*Putting powder and balls in pocket, and going.*] Yes, yes, I hear you.   [*Near door.*

Ali Then you will promise—even in spite of Pauline?

Bar [*Stops and turns.*] Why in spite of Pauline?

Ali [*Lowering her voice.*] Because I fear that Pauline—[*Indicating her chamber.*] Sh! she may hear us. I fear she will be dreadfully opposed to my marriage.

Bar [*Looking at her.*] And why?

Ali [*Seating herself c., and beckoning him to descend.*] Why? this is between us, is it not? Because I believe that Pauline don't like him much!

Bar [*Descending and finally sitting by her.*] You believe that—but what makes you think so.?

Ali Oh, a thousand little things. When we first met him Pauline was very amiable with him. She welcomed him to our house very graciously, and I was so happy. Then, all at once, after a week or so, and why I never knew, all changed. She received him still with politeness, but no more. Twenty times he called on us in the middle of the day, and Pauline told the servant to say that "the ladies have gone out to walk," when the fact was the ladies were both at home, and one of them was awfully vexed at it, I can tell you. But I didn't dare to say anything. But that wasn't all. The worst was on our departure. [*Stopping and getting up.*] I weary you with my little story?

Bar No, no.

Ali Imagine then, one beautiful morning—at this very hour—Pauline awoke me, saying, "Aline, we must go!" "What, right off?" "Right off." Well, you may think I had a heavy heart, for we had just made up for that day a glorious picnic in the woods, and Hector was to be with us. So I said to sister, "At least, let us write to him and notify him!" It was useless. I took twice as long to dress, I was so vexed, and Pauline hurrying me all the time. As we were getting into our carriage, for the purpose of enabling him to follow us I asked Pauline, as loud as I could, before the servants at the door, "Which way are we going?" and she whispered, "Bagnieres;" but I was not to be foiled, so I said, "What, that dirty Bagnieres!" Just so! [*Very loud.*] Well, indeed we did take the road to Bagnieres, but half way—chu! whisk! we turned off to the left, and away we went to Baste; just as if she was determined obstinately to throw him off the track.

Bar [*Face brightening.*] Yes, yes.

Ali In fact it was a flight!

Bar Yes—yes—a flight. [*Aside.*] Just as she told me.

Ali Then I said to myself, What is to be done? For it was plain she had taken an aversion to him. That was to be seen, since the further we got from him, the happier she became—she laughed, she sang. Oh, dear.

Bar [*Happy.*] That was so.

Ali Yes, and I was very sad—for I said to myself, "I shall see him no more," and I did not, until yesterday, when we met, and he told me he was the son of our neighbor, and then I thought, we are saved, because the Baron will help me! [*Coaxing.*] For he can be so good when he wants to. And then to enable Hector to—[*Stopping.*] but ain't you tired?

Bar No, no, go on, dear little one—go on.

Ali Well, to help him to get into the park by the shortest way, I gave him—now, don't scold me—I was a little foolish—

Bar Say on—you gave him what?

Ali My little key.

Bar Your key?

Ali Yes, of the little green gate.

Bar It was you then, not Pauline?

Ali Pauline?

Bar No, no! what am I saying? [*Aside.*] They spoke truly then She fled from him, and there was no rendezvous.

Ali What are you mumbling about?

Bar Nothing. Go on, my child. Well, he took the key, then—

Ali And he came—[*Blushing*]—yesterday evening.

Bar Ah! you know that he came.

Ali I should think so; he nearly scared me out of my wits.

Bar Then you saw him!

Ali [*Quickly, and innocently.*] Yes, but nobody else did.

Bar You are sure?

Ali Oh, yes, I was all alone. Pauline was on the terrace.

Bar Pauline did not see him?

Ali No! and I'm glad she didn't, for he acted like a crazy man. Once here, he didn't want to go away. I said to him, "Suppose Pauline should come," and he said, "Bother Pauline! who cares for Pauline?"

Bar And then—

Ali And I said over and over again, "It is very wrong," "It is very wrong," and looked so vexed and grieved, that he was touched with my tears, and then—[*Stopping.*]—you see I tell you all, from the moment you promised to be on our side.

Bar I will aid you ; but go on, dear child, go on.

Ali And then he said, " Yes, you are right, Aline, I am guilty, a hundred times more so than you think—"

Bar He said that?

Ali Yes, and I didn't know very well what he meant.

Bar Never mind, I know very well what he meant. Then—go on—

Ali "But,"—this is he speaking all the time, you know,—"but you are an angel, Aline, and you have saved me."

Bar Ah ! he said that, too?

Ali Yes, he said that too, and that's another thing that I didn't very well understand.

Bar I understand, I understand ! Finally—

Ali Finally, he said, "Aline, take back your little key. Innocent accomplice of my fault, take it back, it burns me."

Bar Your key !

Ali Yes.

Bar He gave it back ?

Ali Yes ; see, here it is.

Bar Ah ! that was very well, very well.

Ali Wasn't it? Oh, he's an angel of goodness! and I didn't want to take it back, and I said to him, " No, keep it to come again to-morrow, in open day," and he said, " No, I will not enter this house again, save as an honest man, by the great door, and to demand your hand in marriage." That I understood, you know.

Bar [*Radiant.*] And I too! I understand all !

Ali [*Pouting.*] You comprehend everything ! You are very fortunate.

Bar Yes, fortunate, darling angel, and happy! happy for your sake, for his, for hers. I am very happy !

[*Embraces her, and at the same instant a pistol shot is heard.*

Ali [*Jumping.*] Oh ! What is that.

Bar [*Surprised.*] A shot ! in the park !   [*Goes up quickly.*

PAULINE *enters from chamber, pale, agitated,—does not see the* BARON.

Pau Aline! did you hear?

Ali Yes, it was a shot.   [*Goes up.*

Pau They are fighting ! My husband ! [*Is about to run without having the strength, and in turning finds herself face to face with* BARON, *who comes down on hearing her cry.*] Thank Heaven ! you are safe ! [*Falls.*

Bar [*Clasping her.*] Pauline ! my darling ! my wife !

Pau Ah ! you believe me now !

Bar [*Putting his fingers on her lips.*] Yes, I believe you. But, before Aline, silence!

MACAIRE *appears on threshold, seeking* HECTOR.

Mac Baron! My son! Where is my son?
Bar Your son? [*To himself, as if struck with a sudden idea.*] That shot!
Mac [*Down* c.] Where is he?
Bar I do not know. He is in the park. [MACAIRE *goes toward* ALINE. BARON *seizes the letter left by* HECTOR, *on table.*] That letter! For you, Pauline. [*He opens it, and reads in a low voice:*] "Forgive me the evil I have done, madame, I am punished!"
Pau Ah!
Bar [*Stops, takes her hand, and pursues reading in a tremulous voice.*] Your husband would not believe the word of the living, perhaps he will believe the word of the dead, who signs your innocence with his blood." Ah! the unfortunate!
Pau He has killed himself!
Bar It was my fault. I was merciless.
Mac Baron, he was with you! That letter!
Bar It is not for you.
Mac [*Striving to take it.*] It is from him.
Bar You shall not see it!
Mac [*Going up* c.] My son! Where is he? Hector! Hector!
Hec [*Outside.*] Father!
Ali He is coming, see!

HECTOR *enters, followed by* FLIBBARD, GRANCHOU, *who has his jaw tied up, and black eye, and patch across the nose, and all the villagers,*—ALINE *and* PAULINE *together, down* R.

Hec Father! Aline!   [*Embraces his father, and they go across scene.*
Mac My son!
Flib Your son! He is a bloodthirsty miscreant! Mr. Mayor,—myself, and the members of the Common Council were secreted in the park, when along came this Guy Fawkes, with a pistol, and a pocket full of powder and shot, out of which, like a Brutus, he is loading the infernal instrument. We spring upon him from behind, and off goes the contents in Granchou's jaw. We seize him, like Cataline, and here he is, like Spartacus, and this makes the fourth time since yesterday, that I have saved the country, like—like—Washington; and Granchou bleeds for his native land.
                            [GRAN. *mumbles some words.*
Bar What does he say?
Flib I think he says that his native land may go to the devil!
Bar Never mind, Granchou shall be next mayor.
Flib And now, Mr. Baron, all these good people demand to know what is to be the fate of this assassin—this—
Bar Well, what I propose, is, that we chain him up for the remainder of his miserable existence.

Flib [*To his fellow-patriots.*] Good !   [HECTOR *a step forward.*

Bar [*Going to* ALINE, *and bringing her to* C., *beckoning* HECTOR.] And it is this pretty jailer who shall hold the chains.

All [*Stupefied.*] Ah !

Hec Ah, sir !

Flib My friends, we have not been saving our native land ? We have only been making a match.

Bar Exactly ! [GRANCHOU *mumbles something.*] What does he say ?

Flib [*Who has severely reprimanded* GRANCHOU *in dumb show, then aloud, blandly.*] He says that virtue is its own reward.

All Long live the Mayor !

Ali [*To* BARON.] You hear my recruits ?   [BARON *bows.*

Hec So I have a rare little politician for a wife ? Then we will make a board of Aldermen at home, of which you shall be chairman, and I,—for I don't deserve anything better—will be sergeant-at-arms.

Ali Then come to order. Order! All persons stirring will be turned out. I've a word to say. Perhaps you think he doesn't deserve to be so happy ; but then if the men only got what they deserved, we should never get the men. What should a girl do? Not fall in love till she has demanded her beau's references from his last place ? That would not be love, it would be common sense, which is a different thing. So I think that, after all, if we only love well, something or somebody will take care of the rest.

THE END.